D1430861

Welcome to ALADDIN QUIX!

If you are looking for fast, fun-to-read stories with colorful characters, lots of kid-friendly humor, easy-to-follow action, entertaining story lines, and lively illustrations, then **ALADDIN QUIX** is for you!

But wait, there's more!

If you're also looking for stories with tables of contents; word lists; about-the-book questions; 64, 80, or 96 pages; short chapters; short paragraphs; and large fonts, then **ALADDIN QUIX** is *definitely* for you!

ALADDIN QUIX: The next step between ready to reads and longer, more challenging chapter books, for readers five to eight years old.

HARVEY HAMMER

Class Pest

BY
Davy Ocean

ILLUSTRATED
BY
Aaron Blecha

ALADDIN QUIX

New York London Toronto Sydney New Delhi

ALADDIN QUIX
Simon & Schuster Children's Publishing Division
1230 Avenue of the Americas, New York, New York 10020
First Aladdin QUIX hardcover edition May 2023
Text copyright © 2023 by Working Partners Limited
Illustrations copyright © 2023 by Aaron Blecha
Class Pest is a Working Partners book.
Also available in an Aladdin QUIX paperback edition.

For information about special discounts for bulk purchases, please contact
Simon & Schuster Special Sales at 1-866-506-1949 or business@simonandschuster.com.
The Simon & Schuster Speakers Bureau can bring authors to your live event.
For more information or to book an event contact the Simon & Schuster Speakers
Bureau at 1-866-248-3049 or visit our website at www.simonspeakers.com.
Designed by Karin Paprocki
The illustrations for this book were rendered digitally.
The text of this book was set in Archer Medium.
Manufactured in the United States of America 0323 LAK
2 4 6 8 10 9 7 5 3 1
Library of Congress Control Number 2022948893
ISBN 9781534455160 (hc)
ISBN 9781534455153 (pbk)
ISBN 9781534455177 (ebook)

With special thanks to Paul Ebbs

Cast of Characters

Ms. Lumpy: Harvey's teacher

Harvey Hammer: Young hammerhead shark

Spike: Puffer fish classmate and Harvey's enemy

Rocky: Barnacle classmate and Spike's best friend

Flash: Turtle classmate

Pirate: The class pet parrotfish

Hettie: Harvey's older sister

Mom Hammer, aka Hanna: Chief of police; mother of Hettie, Harvey, and Finn

Dad Hammer: Father of Hettie, Harvey, and Finn

Finn: Harvey's baby brother

Bluey: Whalebus driver

Sea J. Marsh-shallow: Famous DJ from Coral Cove

Pearl: Racing clam classmate

Sandy: Sand shark classmate

Connie: Crab classmate

Contents

1

Class Pet Problem

FOOOOOOOOOOOOOM!

Iron-Manta-Ray zoomed down from the sea surface, a trail of atomic bubbles behind him. As he landed on the seabed, he slammed into the evil Shelby McSkullop's

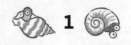

team of supervillain scallops.

The scallop bad guys needed to be rounded up. If they weren't, they'd cause more and more trouble on the low seas!

Hammer-Boy, Iron-Manta-Ray's sidekick, unhooked the NET-O-MATIC fishing system from his Utilit-Sea Belt and prepared to activate it. But then . . .

"Ms. Lumpy, look at **Harvey**; he's drawing again!" The voice of my sometimes friend, sometimes enemy **Spike** cut across my hammer-ears.

 3

I felt my eyes bulging as I full-on **goggled**, which made me lift my gaze from the paper where I'd been sketching the final **installment** of my *Iron-Manta-Ray versus the Seaverse!* comic.

I really like drawing comics and want to be a famous comic book artist one day, so I practice whenever and wherever I can.

"He's drawing goofy pictures in his notebook again, Ms. Lumpy," Spike said.

Spike is a puffer fish. When he's excited, he puffs up like a balloon, and long horrible spikes stick out of him. His best friend is a barnacle named **Rocky**. And they love to give me trouble.

"Harvey Hammer, what have I

told you about paying attention in class?" asked Ms. Lumpy, our sea cucumber teacher. She looked at me over the top of her glasses. And she didn't look happy.

I know I should have been concentrating on the lesson, but it was almost the end of class. I think Ms. Lumpy was asking if anyone wanted to take care of the class pet for the weekend.

No way, I thought. What I *really* wanted to do for the weekend was finish my comic that night so I

could go to my turtle friend **Flash**'s birthday party the next day. I had been waiting all week for the party, and nothing was going to stop me from going.

"Well, Harvey, don't you think it's more important to listen in class than doodle in your notebook?" Ms. Lumpy asked.

"But, Ms. Lumpy," I tried to explain, "my Iron-Manta-Ray comic is the best one yet. I'm going to be famous one day, Ms. Lumpy."

Everyone in class was as silent

as a clam, but all of a sudden a loud voice **squawked**, **"I'M GOING TO BE F-A-A-A-Y MUSH F-A-AAAA-Y MUSH."**

Everyone turned around and looked at the back of the room. All the cool class pets were there: spiderfish, clown fish, and footballfish. Pets that were creepy or strong or beautiful.

And then there was **Pirate** the parrotfish. He was sitting on his **perch**, ruffling his green fins, and shaking his scaly tail. I thought

he stared right at me, and then he squawked again, **"I'M GOING TO BE F-A-A-A-Y MUSH F-A-AAAA-Y MUSH."**

My hammerhead felt like it had suddenly tied itself into a knot, and all I could hear were the other kids

and squids laughing at my horrified expression.

"Oh no!" I cried.

"Oh yes, Harvey," answered Ms. Lumpy. "As I was saying before while you were drawing, the class pets are being taken home for the weekend by a select few students. I think you would greatly benefit from a little **responsibility**."

She paused and continued, "You will be assigned Pirate the parrotfish."

Spike was laughing so much, he

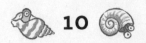

floated over onto his back, kicking his fins in the water.

"I can't take him home, Ms. Lumpy," I pleaded. "I have a party to go to!"

"I have a pa-r-r-ty to go to—awk!" Pirate parroted.

Ms. Lumpy nodded. "Yes. It looks like you *both* have a party to go to."

This was going to be the worst weekend since **Hettie**—my always *perfect* older sister—accidentally dropped her craft glue into my underwear drawer!

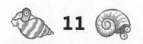

2

Caught Fin-Handed

Mom and **Dad** have a strict no-pets **policy** at our house. It's not that they don't like pets. It's just that with

· my sister, Hettie, who never stops playing her guitar,

- my baby brother, **Finn**, who never stops laughing, crying, and pooping,
- my father, who is always trying to keep our household running smoothly, and
- my police-chief mom, who is always rushing off to answer another siren or alarm to help the citizens of Coral Cove,

our house is as noisy as crashing tidal waves. A pet would only make everything even louder.

It wasn't easy to get Pirate and his perch onto the whalebus. I swung the perch around three times before I got settled in my seat, clunking **Bluey** the driver twice on the back of his head, then thwacking Flash so hard on his turtle shell that it flipped him right over. His little legs kicked like seaweed in a storm.

"See you tomorrow, Harvey, and *only* you at the party," Flash called

when I got off the bus with Pirate.

I quickly snuck him into my house and to my room without making a single sound. My parents *could not* find out that there was a parrotfish here or that he was here because I hadn't been paying attention in class and had been working on my comic.

"Please, please, Pirate, be quiet. I'll give you all the sandy crackers you can eat," I whispered to him.

Amazingly, Pirate listened to me, at first. But just as I was shutting my door—

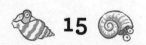

B'doyng, b'doyng, flum, dum, flum, b'doyng.

It was Hettie, playing her guitar. And then she started singing at the top of her gills:

"I like noise,
I like toys,
and my brother Harvey
is an annoying boy."

Before I could stop him, Pirate repeated everything Hettie had done at the top of his gills.

"B'doyng, b'doyng, flum,

dum, flum, b'doyng.

I like noise,

I like toys,

and my brother Harvey

is an annoying boy."

"Stop it! Please stop!" I hissed, hoping no one would hear him.

But the only reply I got was Pirate making guitar noises and singing again.

"Shhhhh, shhhhhh, shhhhh," I said.

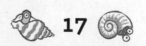 17

"Pirate want a cracker? Pirate want a cracker?"

It didn't help.

"Harvey, is that you? Since when did you start singing?" My mother came into my room, followed by my father—who was holding Finn, as usual—and then Hettie, who was

still holding her guitar under her fin.

"Who is that?" my mother asked, pointing her fin at Pirate. It looked like steam was beginning to come out of her ears. "You know we don't allow pets."

"It's . . . it's . . . the class pet. I have to take care of him for the weekend."

My father wiped some gross goo from Finn's mouth and asked, "How come? Is it a special prize?"

My eyes lit up. "Yes." I nodded. "A prize. That's what it is."

"Well, that's wonderful," my mom said.

"That's wun-her-fuuuuul—awk," Pirate squawked.

Hettie giggled. "He sounds just like you, Mom." Dad and I laughed too. Pirate did do a good Mom impression.

"Jussssssst like you, Mommmm—

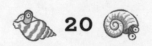

awk," said Pirate in Hettie's voice.

I knew I couldn't tell them the truth about why I had Pirate. He wasn't a prize at all. He was a punishment!

"Come on, Harvey, what was the prize for? What happened in class today?" asked Hettie.

I was thinking of saying that I'd gotten the best score on the math test, or that the prize was for super-fast swim sprinting, when—

"Don't you think it's more impor-tant to listen in class than doodle in

your notebook? I think you would greatly benefit from a little responsibility. You will be assigned Pirate the parrotfish."

Now everyone was looking at Pirate. Even Finn, who had dropped his Pacific-fier from his open mouth.

And then they all looked at me.

3

Two Choices

For the rest of the night Pirate wouldn't stop yapping. He seemed to enjoy repeating what Mom had said when she'd found out the truth about why I'd brought the parrotfish home.

"Flash will just have to celebrate

without you, Harvey. We can't reward you when you've gotten into trouble in class."

"Trouble in class, trouble in class! Awk."

"Please stop reminding me, Pirate," I said as I climbed into my seabed and pulled the blankets over me. Luckily, Pirate settled down too. His snoring was bad, but it wasn't as bad as his squawking.

The next morning my mom and dad called me into the kitchen. Pirate was with me.

"We are still very disappointed in your behavior in class yesterday, Harvey. Do not let us hear about you drawing in your notebook again while you should be listening to Ms. Lumpy."

"Yes, Mom. Yes, Dad," I answered.

"However," my dad continued, "we

have come up with a fun way for you to be even more responsible."

I gulped. *Even more responsible? Fun? That sounds awful,* I thought.

Mom smiled at Dad, and he smiled back.

"Would you still like to go to Flash's party today?" Mom asked.

I couldn't believe my ears. **"Yes, of course I would!"**

My dad nodded at my mom and said, "You can go to the party as long as you bring Pirate with you."

"What?" I cried. "He'll ruin everything! And Flash told me *not* to bring him."

"Well, Harvey. You have a decision to make, don't you?" Dad said. "Either stay home with Pirate. Or go to the party with Pirate."

"Go to the party with Pirate, with Pirate, with Pirate. Awk, awk," the parrotfish squawked loudly.

I hurried to my room with that annoying pest nipping my fins.

With my sister's guitar sounding as loud as a tidal wave, I tried to think about my choices.

STAY HOME WITH PIRATE

· Try to finish my Iron-Manta-Ray comic, with

Pirate squawking all afternoon.

· Not be able to finish my Iron-Manta-Ray comic

due to Pirate squawking all afternoon.

GO TO FLASH'S BIRTHDAY PARTY WITH PIRATE

· Go to the biggest birthday party of my entire life

and have the most awesome time ever.

· Pretend that Pirate isn't with me while I have the

most amazing time ever.

I really didn't have a choice.

There was no way I was going to

miss wishing Flash a happy birthday.

"Harvey, Pirate, time to go!"
Hettie yelled to us.

It was bad enough that Pirate had
to go to the party, but Hettie? It sure
seemed like Flash had invited anyone who could swim in Coral Cove.

At three o'clock sharp Dad dropped
all three of us off at Flash's house.
Before we swam out of the fish-auto,
he stopped me.

"Remember, Harvey," he warned,

"Pirate is *your* responsibility. You decided to come to the party, and while that might mean having fun, it also means taking care of Pirate."

I tried not to roll my eyes while Dad was talking.

My plan was to park Pirate in one corner of Flash's living room with a huge pile of sea salt parrotfish crackers to keep him happy— and to keep his mouth filled so he wouldn't get in my way with all his squawking.

"Yes, Dad. I hear you. Everything

will be fine," I answered. Pirate had to chime in, of course.

"Everything will be f-iiii-nnnne. **AWK.**"

It better be, Pirate, I said to myself.

4

Party Time

When we swam through the front door of Flash's sea turtle house, we were **awed**.

Famous DJ **Sea J. Marsh-shallow** was blasting music. It looked like the whole school was there, dancing

up a deep-sea storm! Glow-squid disco lanterns were shining, and the blue-silver light of the lantern fish was **pulsing** in time to the music.

Sea J. Marsh-shallow stood behind two massive turntables, and everyone's favorite song was playing.

"I love the ocean foamy foam.
No longer do I want to roamy roam.
The open seas are my homey home.
My homey, homey home."

WOW! WOW! WOW! I was so glad I had decided to come to the party. It was amazing!

And then Pirate opened his beak:

"The open ssssssssssssseas are my homey hommmmmmmmme—awk! My homey, homey home—awk!"

And every single head in the room turned to stare at me.

No one made a peep.

Flash zoomed over to my side.

"Harvey," he whispered. "I asked you *not* to bring Pirate!"

"I'm so sorry, Flash. I didn't want to miss your birthday, and my parents said I couldn't go unless

I brought the class pet," I said. "I promise he won't get in the way. I've got an entire bag of sea salt crackers to keep him stuffed and silent."

But Flash didn't look **convinced**.

"Please, please, please. **Let us stay!**" I pleaded. "This is the coolest party I've ever been invited to."

I guess begging worked, because Flash kind of shrugged his shell and nodded. I was starting to take Pirate over to a corner of the room when Sea J. Marsh-shallow tapped the microphone with one of his legs.

He cleared his throat and began,
"Flash, I know there is no way you
could know this, but I am violently
allergic to parrotfish." He looked at

me, pointed straight at Pirate, and continued, "I will have to leave your birthday celebration immediately. Happy birthday, Flash."

The DJ waved to Flash and raced out of the house.

Once again every single head in the room turned to stare at me.

"Great, Harvey!" shouted Spike. "Now you've gone and ruined Flash's party. Thanks for nothing!"

"Thanks for noth-innnnng—awk," repeated Pirate.

Before I knew what was happening, all the kids and squids had surrounded me and Pirate.

Rocky said, "You know what time it is, Harvey? Time to go."

My classmates **Pearl**, **Sandy**, and **Connie** chimed in, "And don't forget to bring that pesky pet with you!"

And then Hettie swam over. "Does that mean I have to go home *too*? Wait until I tell Mom and Dad what happened. Not very responsible of you, was it, Harvey?"

Oh no!

Hettie was right. What would

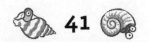

my mom and dad say? Pirate had ruined Flash's party, and now he was about to ruin my life.

Forever.

5

To the Rescue

As I reached for Pirate's perch, he flew off and headed straight to all the DJ equipment Sea J. Marsh-shallow had left behind.

What is he doing now? I worried.

"Come on, Pirate. Please stop

playing around. We've got to go."

But what he did next was incredible, and it took everyone by surprise.

Especially me.

He turned the disco lights back on, took over the turntables, and . . .

"We've got to go.

We're saying, 'So loooooooooong.'

But not before

I sing this soooooooooong.

Flash the turtle is

the best bud in the seeeeeeeea,

Especially for

my friend Harveeeeeeey.

Let's get this party rocking,

rolling, and moooooooooving.

Let's dance all night,

shaking and grooooooooooving!

AWWWWK!"

At first no one **uttered** a sound.

And then the party **erupted**.

Everyone started cheering, **"Go, Pirate! Go, Pirate!"** at the top of their gills, singing along and dancing.

I glanced over at Flash, who looked like he was in a state of electric-eel shock. I quickly floated over to him and nudged him toward the front of the crowd.

Hettie came over to us and started singing, **"Go, Flash! Go, Flash!"** and everyone else joined in.

Flash was moving to the beat with some of his favorite dance moves: the Shell, the Backstroke, the Wavy Gravy. I had never seen him look so happy.

And just like that, Flash's birthday bash turned around and went from awful to awesome. The party was saved from being a mega disaster,

and I was saved from being a laughingstock shark at school and being in mega trouble with my mom and dad.

And it was all thanks to the most annoying, loudmouthed, pesky, wonderful, lifesaving class pet—my new friend Pirate the parrotfish!

Once we were back home in my room, I scratched Pirate's head with my fin while I worked on my comic.

Iron-Manta-Ray called to Hammer-Boy, "Who is that with you, Hammer?

 49

You know we've got to catch Shelby McSkullop once and for all."

"It's Pirate the Pulverizer! He's my new super sidekick, and no evil supervillain can match his powers. Right, PP?"

"You said it, HB! **AWWWK!**"

Word List

allergic (uh•LER•jik): Having a bodily reaction, such as sneezing or itching, to something

awed (AWD): Filled with wonder

convinced (kuhn•VINST): Certain

erupted (ih•RUP•ted): Became suddenly active

goggled (GAH•guld): Stared with wide eyes

installment (in•STAWL•munt): One part of an ongoing story

perch (PURCH): A bar on which a bird sits

policy (PAH•luh•see): A set of rules as a guide

pulsing (PUHL•sing): Going off and on rhythmically

responsibility (rih•spahn•suh•BIH•luh•tee): A duty to take care of something

squawked (SKWAWKT): Screamed harshly

uttered (UH•terd): Spoke a word or sent out as a sound

Questions

1. Why did Ms. Lumpy make Harvey take Pirate the parrotfish home? What was he supposed to learn from taking care of Pirate?

2. What instrument does Harvey's sister, Hettie, play?

3. Who is the hero of Harvey's comic book? Who is the supervillain?

4. Why did Sea J. Marsh-shallow have to leave Flash's party?

5. How did Pirate save the day?